Max's Special Spring

Max & Ruby

Grosset & Dunlap
An Imprint of Penguin Group (USA) LLC

penguin.com
A Penguin Random House Company

From an episode of the animated television series *Max & Ruby*.
Series © 2011–2012 M&R V Productions Ltd. All rights reserved.

Penguin supports copyright. Copyright fuels creativity, encourages diverse voices, promotes free speech, and creates a vibrant culture. Thank you for buying an authorized edition of this book and for complying with copyright laws by not reproducing, scanning, or distributing any part of it in any form without permission. You are supporting writers and allowing Penguin to continue to publish books for every reader.

Max & Ruby © Rosemary Wells. Licensed by Nelvana Limited. NELVANA is a registered trademark of Nelvana Limited. CORUS is a trademark of Corus Entertainment Inc. All rights reserved. Published in 2015 by Grosset & Dunlap, a division of Penguin Young Readers Group, 345 Hudson Street, New York, New York 10014. GROSSET & DUNLAP is a trademark of Penguin Group (USA) LLC. Manufactured in China.

ISBN 978-0-448-48453-2

10 9 8 7 6 5 4 3 2 1

W9-ALK-094

"It's almost spring, Max!" said Max's sister, Ruby. "But look at how messy our yard is. Let's clean up and compost."

"Compost?" said Max.

"Yes, Max. Composting is just like recycling. Everything has to be reused. And maybe the birds will come back once we get the yard ready for springtime!"

Max wasn't interested in cleaning up the yard.
He wanted to play with his dump truck and crane.

Ruby picked up twigs.

Max came over with his dump truck.

"Take this pile of sticks, Max," said Ruby, "and drive it to the compost heap."

But Max didn't know where the compost heap was.

"*Vroom, vroom!*" said Max.

Max dumped the twigs under the tree.
There were birds in the tree.
"Birds!" said Max.

8

Ruby raked leaves.

Max drove his dump truck back to Ruby.
"Leaves go in the compost pile, too, Max!" said Ruby.
"*Chug, chug, chug!*" said Max.

Max dumped the leaves next to the twigs.

Ruby found old grapevines in the garden.
They looked like strings. She rolled them into a ball.

"Can you put these grapevines in the compost pile, too, Max?" said Ruby.

Max used his crane to pick up the grapevines.
"*Clank, clank, clank!*" said Max.

Max dumped the grapevines next to the leaves and twigs.
"*Peep, peep!*" tweeted the birds up in the tree.

Next, Ruby cleaned out the birdbath.
"The birds might need to take a bath after the long winter," said Ruby.

Max dug a hole in the garden so the birds could find worms to eat.

Ruby filled up the bird feeder.

"I hope the birds can find a place to live in our yard," said Ruby.

Just then, Ruby and Max saw that the birds had taken twigs, leaves, and grapevines from Max's piles and had made a nest out of them in the tree!

"Recycle!" said Max.